Bella's Busy Day

BY MICHÈLE DUFRESNE

Pioneer Valley Educational Press, Inc.

Look at me!

I am running.

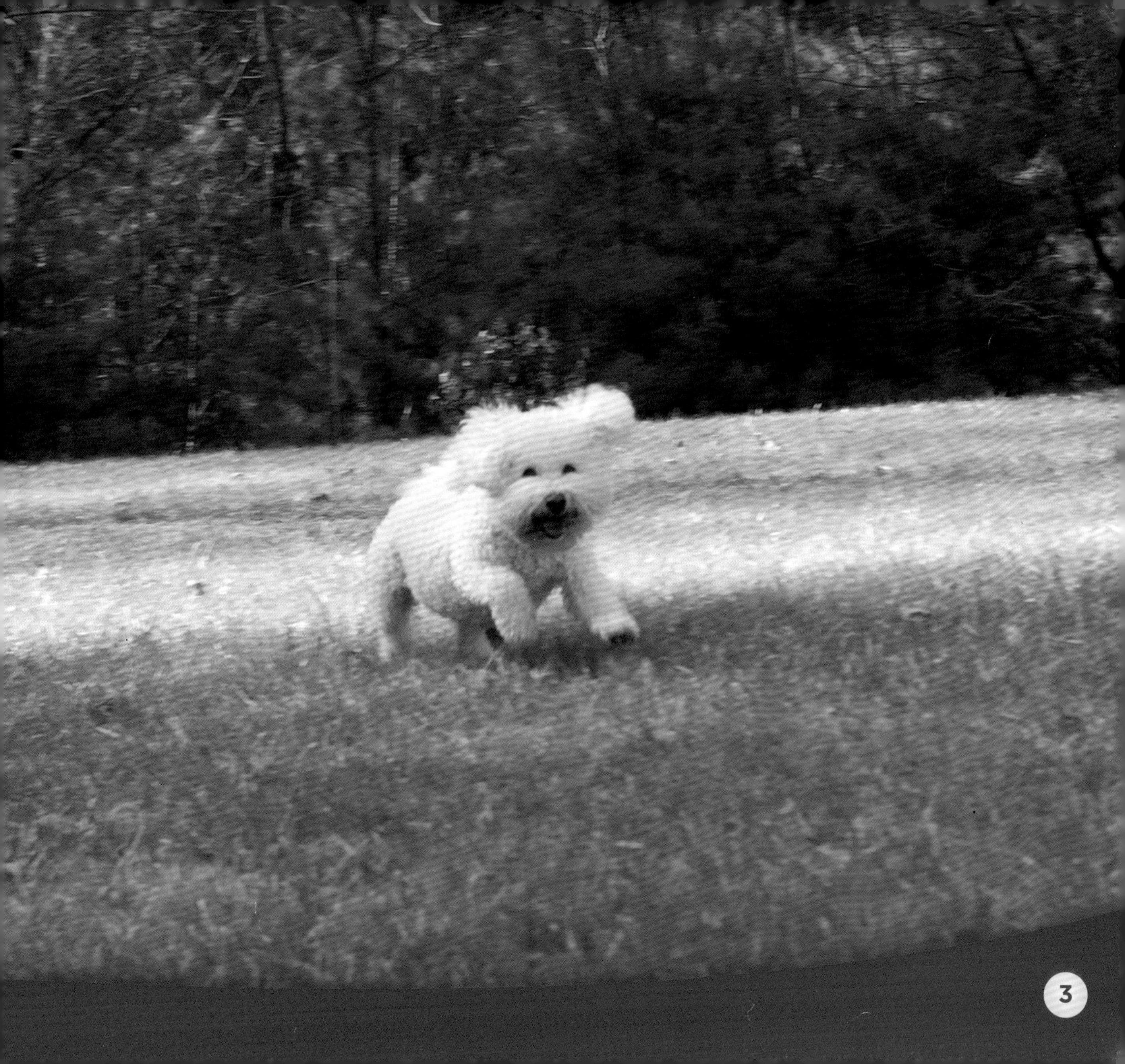

Look at me!

I am jumping.

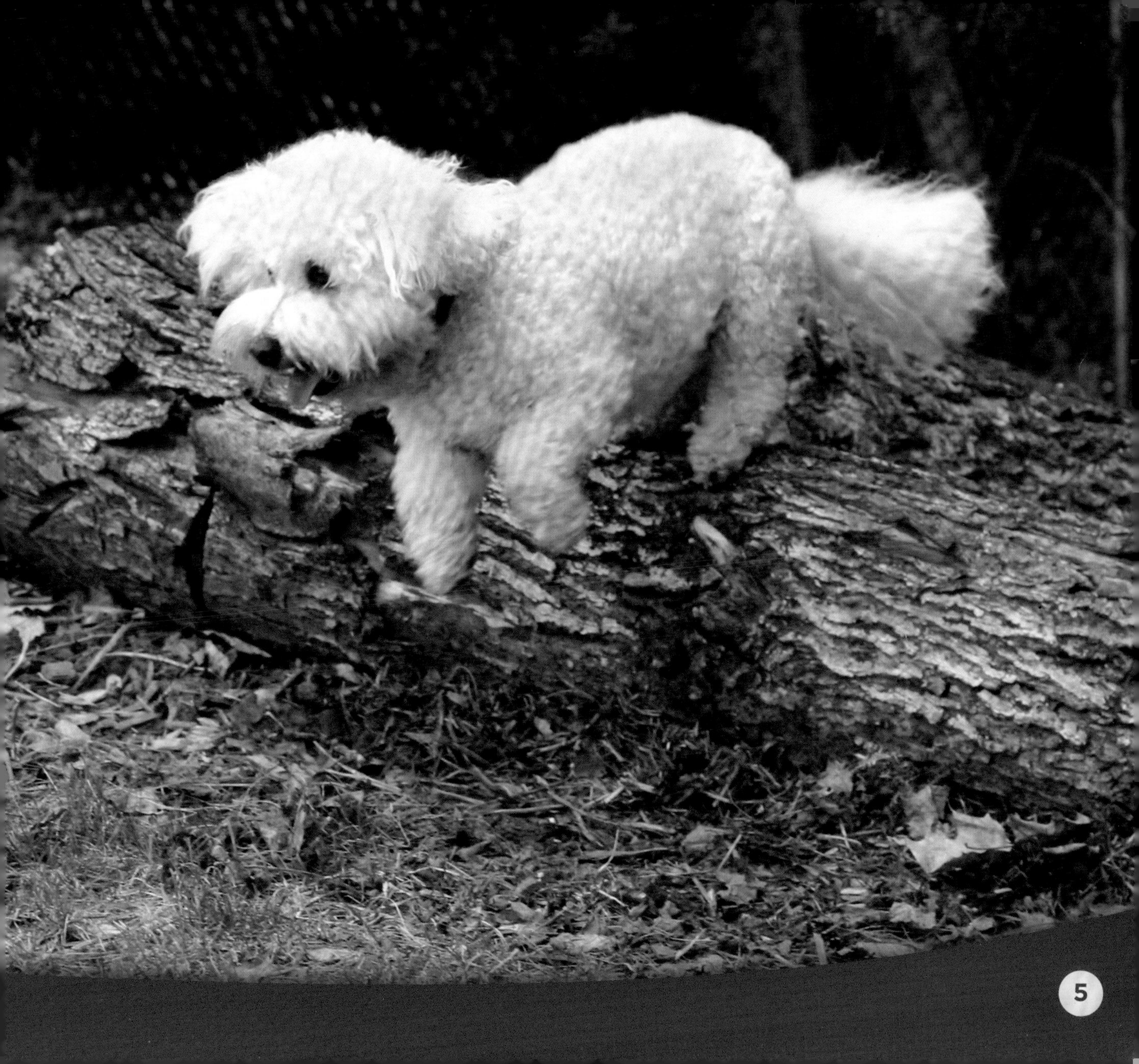

Look at me!
I am walking.

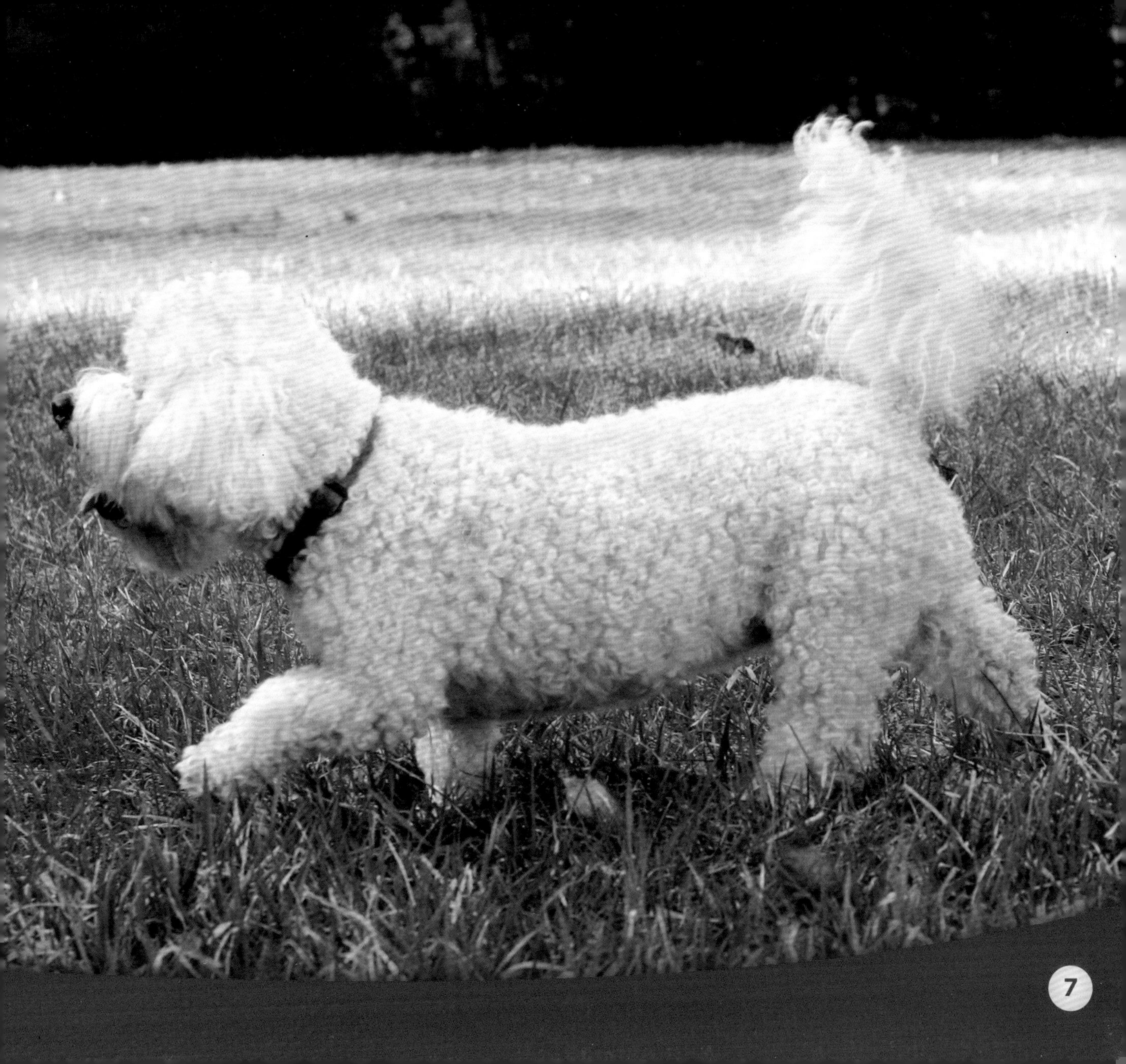

Look at me!
I am swimming.

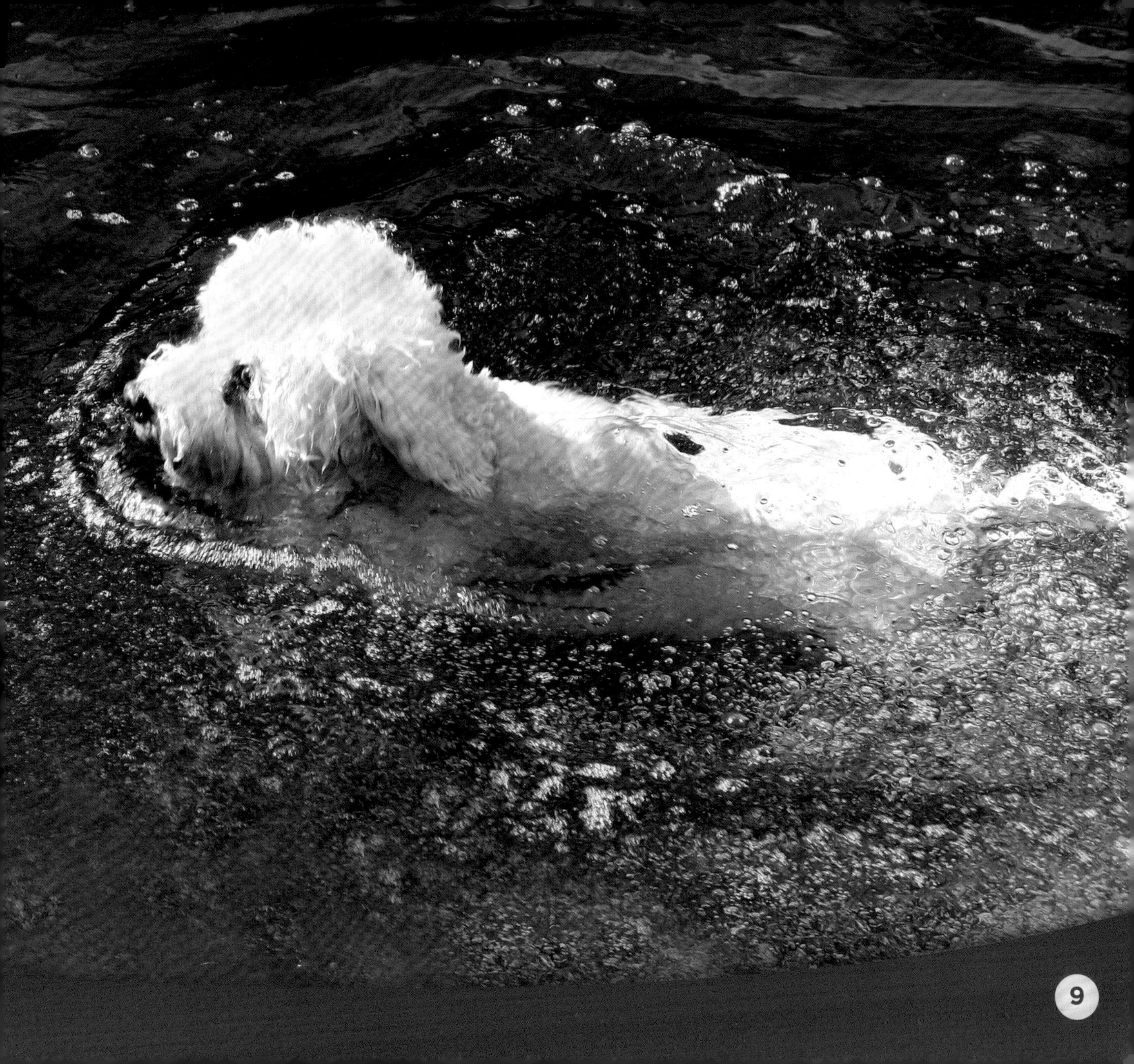

Look at me!
I am sitting.

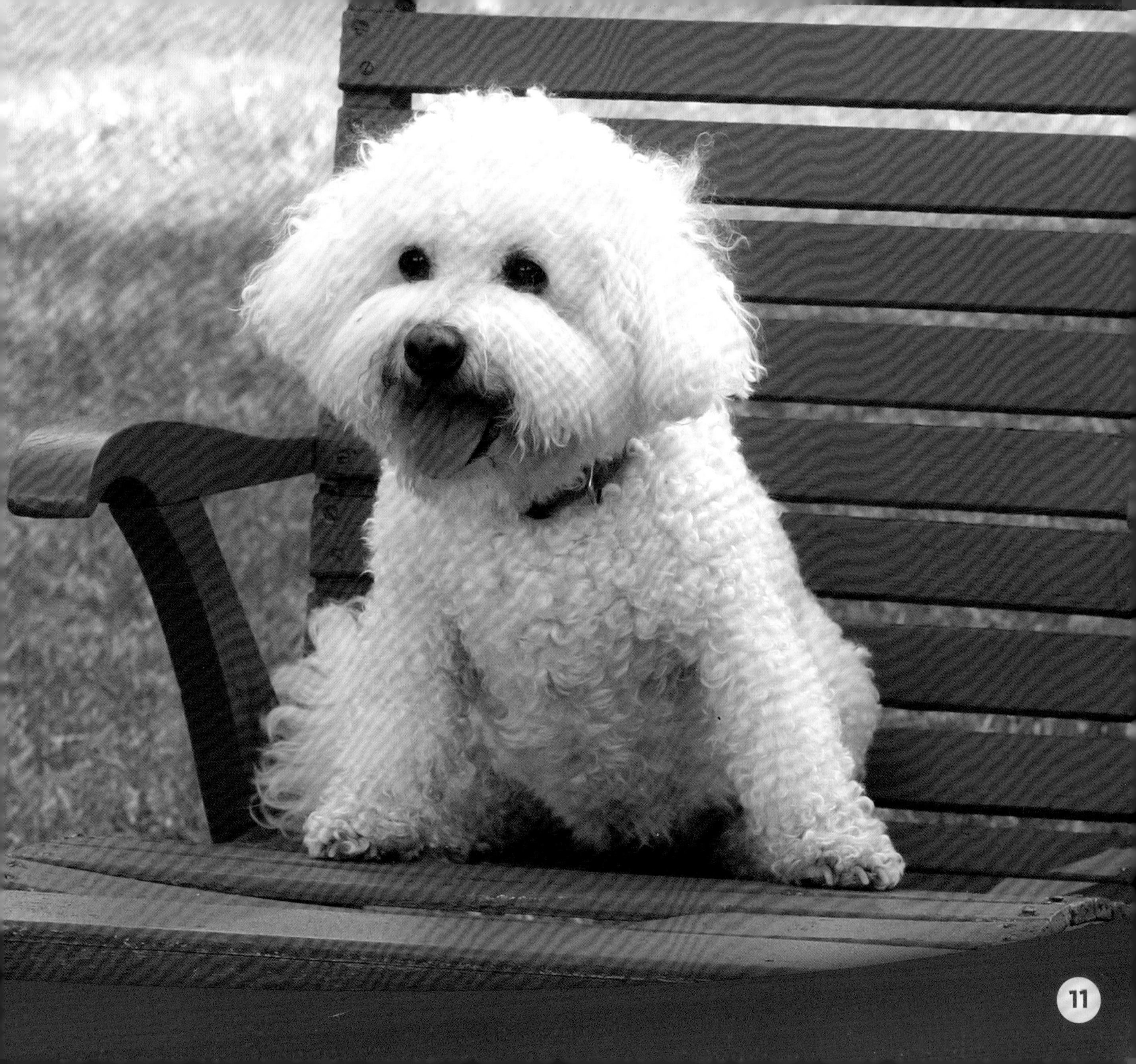

Look at me!

I am napping.

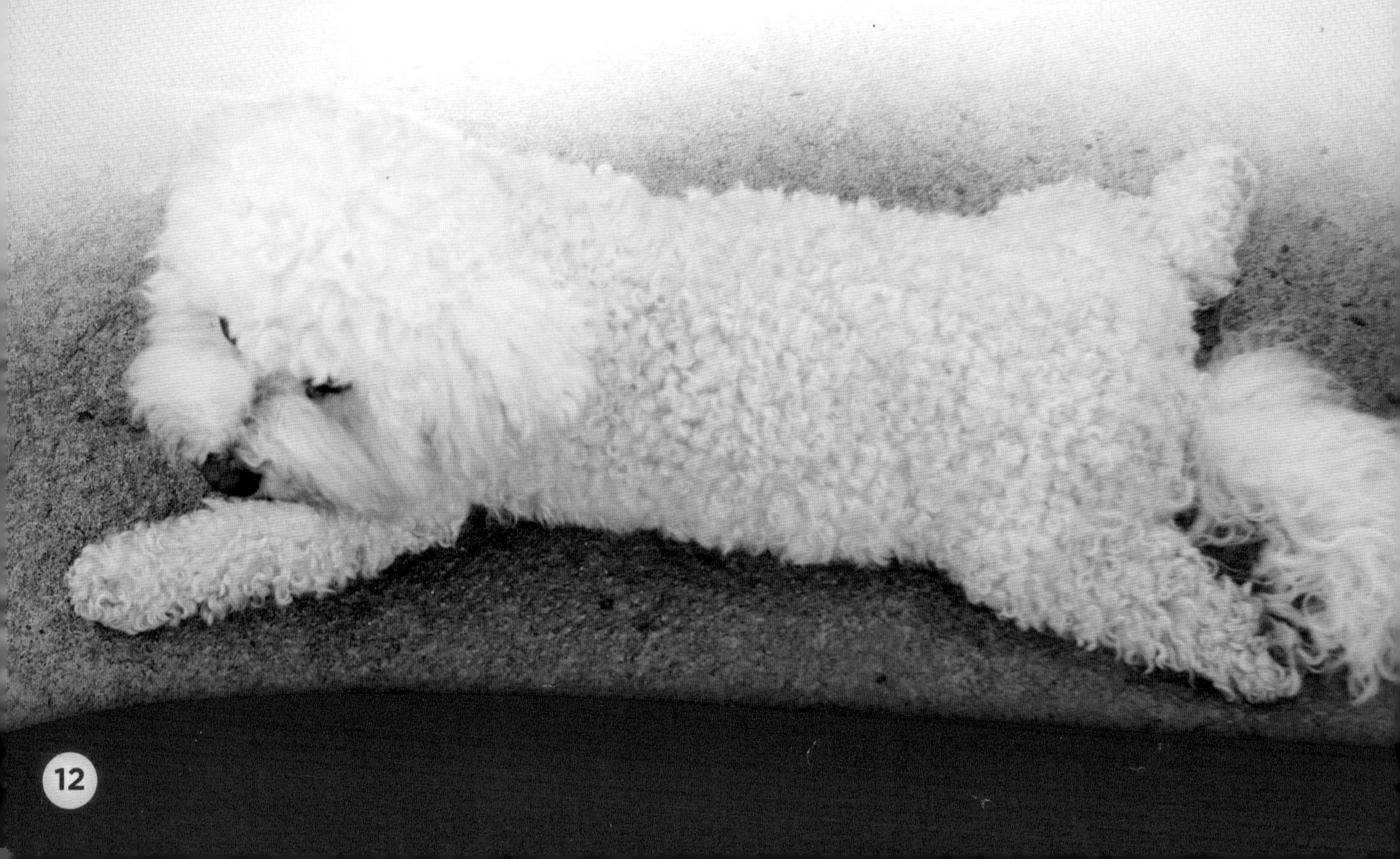